Photography contributed by Rico Torres, Nels Israelson, and Robert Rodriguez

Library of Congress catalog card number: 2003103537
Printed in the U.S.A.
Book design by Joe Merkel

1 2 3 4 5 6 7 8 9 10
❖
First Edition

www.harperchildrens.com
www.spykids.com

How to Be a Spy Kid

ADAPTED BY KATE EGAN
BASED ON THE SCREENPLAY BY
ROBERT RODRIGUEZ

HarperFestival®
A Division of HarperCollins*Publishers*

So you want to be a spy kid?

We can show you how!

We are Carmen and Juni Cortez, two of the best kid spies in the business.

We go on top secret missions.

We have saved the world a few times, too.

When we were new to the job,

we learned a few things from books.

But we learned a lot more in action.

That's because we were in action

all the time!

Here's what you need to know to

be a spy kid.

Spy kids need to be brave.

You can't be afraid of anything

when you are undercover.

Spy kids need to be tough.

You never know when—or who—

you will have to fight.

Spy kids need to move really fast!
Sometimes we chase bad guys.
Sometimes we are chased by bad guys.
Every minute counts when you're
in danger.

Spy kids get to drive amazing vehicles (even though we are too young to drive cars).

It helps to be calm behind the controls— especially if you are underwater.

Or in the air.

A good sense of direction
comes in handy.
Spy missions will take you
to many places.

You'll need to figure out
how to get around.
You'll need to know what
to do if you get lost.

Spy kids must be able to spot bad
guys in disguise.

Spy kids sometimes wear disguises,
too—like this one.

It makes us look just like regular kids!
We can go anywhere dressed like this.

Spy kids have to be ready for
anything—or anybody.
Spy kids even have to be ready for
bad guys without bodies!
These skeletons were no match for us.

Spy kids always hope for the best.

But we are always prepared

for the worst.

That's why we carry lots of gadgets.

Some are high-tech, like RALPH.

Some are low-tech, too.

Uncle Machete gave us some

Elastic Wonders.

They are really just rubber bands.

But the best gadgets

can be very simple.

Spy kids have to make

the best of things.

If Plan A doesn't work,

you need to think up a Plan B fast.

One time our gadgets failed us

and we had to start a fire with a stick!

Having fun is a big part of

being a spy kid.

You'll need to be good at that, too.

We love going to parties!

And we are not shy on the dance floor.

A good spy can't help having enemies.
Gary and Gerti Giggles are also
spy kids.
We had to trick them when they tried
to take over one of our missions.

It is okay to steer clear of enemies.

But spy kids should always stick
with their partners.

Nobody should have to fall through
a volcano alone.

Here are a few more things
to keep in mind.
Sometimes things are not
what they seem.
Even your family can fool you.
These two kids look like us—
but they're really robots!

23

Once in a while, even the best spies lose their cool.

Look at what happened here!

Spies need to move quietly.

Your partner can help you with this.

We are lucky to come from
a family of spies.
Our mother and father
are very famous in the field.

Our grandparents are
pretty sneaky, too.

But you do not need a spy family
to become a good spy kid.
Here is the most important thing
that you need to do:

You *must* follow our advice!

(That's a joke.

All spy kids should have

a sense of humor.)

Seriously, anybody can be a spy kid.
Even you!

But you can't tell anyone what we told you.

You can't tell where you learned the tricks of the trade.

It is classified information.

And everybody knows

this:

A good spy knows how to keep a secret!